# The Wind and the Sun argued.

"I am the strongest!"

shouted the Wind.

"I am!"

glinted the Sun.

"I bet I can get that man's coat off!"

boasted the Wind.

He tried hard,

but the man just shivered
and held on to his coat.

"I can do better,"
flashed the Sun.

It got hotter and hotter
until the man took off
his coat.

The Wind stormed off and
the Sun just glittered.